R.

MW00938931

13 & some change

SECOND SIGHT PRESS

R. A. Ingram

ISBN-13: 978-0692646502
ISBN-10: 0692646507

Published by Second Sight Press

First edition, February 2016

For Yellow Grandma and Pink Grandma

"Bring me back the change."
"I don't have any left."
Lies
I said it all the time and I never got caught up
Checkin' for others when I should have been checkin' myself
Striving to stay true to myself while defining myself
Change in a teen isn't always accepted
So I kept the extra pocket-change and the change within me to
myself…

-Raindrops

CONTENTS

ACKNOWLEDGMENTS

This collection of vignettes would not have been possible without the help and inspiration of so many. Thank you to my beautiful and supportive wife and soon to be mother of my first child. Thank you Renae for standing by me and cheering me on throughout the entire writing process. I am indebted to my parents, my sisters, and brother who encouraged me to dream big and inspired much of what is written within these pages. Thank you to all of my cousins, aunts, uncles, and friends who shine through many of the characters who shape Keith's development in the story. *Graciás* Paul for your immense support and coaching, I am eternally grateful. I must shout out San Jose, California, the city that raised me and the Bay Area for shaping my experiences, friendships, and this story. I would also like to thank all of my students. This book is a gift from you to me. You all showed me that your stories need to be represented, that the experience of growing up in the Bay Area needs to be represented, for that I say thank you.

BANANA POPSICLES

My mom's side calls me Keif. My dad's side calls me Keith. My names are perfect; they have less syllables than my brother and sisters' names, so it's the first name that everybody calls out when they need something. I really am "the middle" too because Antoinette is only a year older than Mikey and Nikki is five years older than me. People say ,that the middle gets left out; it's not true though. Nikki talks to me because I understand most of what she's talking about, and the younger ones talk to me too because I still know how to have fun.

At Titi Arlene's house, in The Pines, my cousin Qwaun yells, "Mom come out here and see this! Kief can actually do tricks on his skateboard!"

"I believe you. Kief, don't hurt yourself baby," Titi yells from the house but doesn't come out.

"Thass why yo shoes be lookin' tore up bruh, 'cause you be doin all them kickflips and stuff. He like a black Tony Hawk pro-skater." Qwaun always

1

makes everybody laugh. He and I are cousin twins; we all have one except for Nikki. Mom and Titi always talk about how they were pregnant at the same time with us. Qwaun's birthday is in December and mine is in February, so he started school a year before I did.

The ice cream truck always comes through the Pines neighborhood. The Pines is filled with courts and cul de sacs, no through streets except the one that had Jerry's liquor store on it. That's why Jerry's always gets robbed. Whenever the ice cream truck pulls up, we get the same thing, the cheapest Popsicle, the banana twin pop for fifty cents. Qwaun always has money, so he spends 3 or 4 dollars on banana twin pops for whoever is outside, including J.R., the Filipino kid from next door who says he's a Crip.

Titi Arlene's house is a duplex, so when we spend the night, Qwaun turns the volume on the T.V. down all the way and we can hear J.R.'s grandpa yelling through the wall. He drinks beer all day and yells at the T.V. in Tagalog all night. We have to pause the video game because we laugh so hard when J.R.'s grandpa sings or cries to the T.V.. We bury our heads in pillows to keep from making too much noise because we know we will get a whoopin' from Uncle Rick if we wake him up. Once we did get whooped. We kept laughing after Uncle Rick went back to bed. Laughing and crying, crying and laughing with little welts on our thighs.

CHESS

The first week of school is always a chess game between me and my new teachers. There are not a lot of Black people at East Hills Middle School, and most of these teachers don't seem like they've ever taught Black kids before.

Mr. Bardwell, my English teacher, sets up the chess board this year. He said *"Wassup"* to me on the first day of school instead of "good morning" like he did to everyone else as we walked into class. I guess that was his attempt at showing me that *he's down*. I told my best friend from church Jaylen about him, and we made a bet to see how long it would take him to ask me if I played basketball. I said three days, Jay said four. We were both wrong. By the end of the second day he hit me with the basketball question. I knew then that he was a loose cannon. He saw my black skin and decided that he had to get me on his side or else I was going to be his enemy, or a class clown, or whatever other

3

stereotypes about black kids he had in his mind. I responded with what Jay and I agreed our response would be to the basketball question this year, "No I play Lacrosse and do archery."

I was only half lying when I said it. Me and Jaylan got scholarships to YMCA camp this summer and we did do archery for a week. As far as lacrosse is concerned, some cool white boys that we met at camp told us all about it, so I knew enough to answer any questions he might ask afterward. All Bardwell said was, "Oh," and then he had this puzzled look on his face. I could tell that he didn't know whether I was giving him attitude or if I was being serious. Accusing me of being disrespectful would have made him a racist, so "Oh," and head nod was his only response.

Today, I sit in the front row, away from the other various shades of brown sitting in the back of the classroom. The Korean girl sitting next to me doesn't know whether to smile at me or ignore me completely. Mr. Bardwell doesn't know what to do either. I can see him giving me passing glances as he walks back and forth during his lecture about the Holocaust. He seems to be deciding whether or not I have ulterior motives by sitting in the front. I know Bardwell is going to make a move soon. He's asking *"raise your hand if"* questions to find out what the class knows about the Holocaust, and I've raised my hand for every question. He probably thinks I am just trying to draw attention to myself. Finally he makes his move.

"Keith, tell us what you know about Elie Wiesel's book *Night*," he says as he sits on his desk.

My move. "It's a sad story about a boy who survives the holocaust."

His move. "Good, please tell us more." He doesn't think I've read it. I can tell by the way he is crossing his arms and squinting his eyes.

My Move. I think I will draw this out a little bit longer. "He loses his family members at different points in the story." I wait for him to make his next move by crossing my arms and locking my eyes on his.

"Ok, please elaborate Mr. Williams. We are all interested in what you know about this autobiography." I am in his head now. He's calling me by my last name with arms crossed. He stands up from his desk and walks in front of the white board, squaring up as if I'm going to rush him or something. The Korean girl sitting next to me keeps looking back and forth from me to Mr. Bardwell. She can feel the tension, and everyone is waiting for me to make my move. I can't see them, but I know the brown back row is sitting up at attention too. It's like the expectation is for me not to know anything, and I'm some sort of threat if I do. I won't give this teacher the satisfaction of meeting his low expectations.

"Well Mr. Bardwell, *Night* is more of a memoir. It's like a snapshot of parts of his and other people's lives and deaths. The author wanted the world to know about all of the terrible stuff that happened during the Holocaust. He uses Eliezer, the main character, as a window into a combination of experiences. But basically the story starts with Eliezer's family living in Hungary when the Nazi's occupy his neighborhood. The family is forced to live in a ghetto and then end up at a couple of death camps where Eliezer loses all of his family members to death or sorting. Eventually, good old America comes through and frees everybody in the camp. The author's goal was to get people to understand that if you don't do anything when evil is happening around you, then you're just as evil as the people doing it." Check mate.

The bell rings. Mr. Bardwell is the shade of red that white people get when they're angry and embarrassed. He nods his head, and I know for the rest of the year that he probably won't like me, but he's going to respect my mind the same way he does the Korean girl's sitting next to me.

BIG DAD

Everything about Dad is big. We bought him a fitted Yankees hat for his birthday one year, and we had to get it in a size eight. The shiny gold sticker on the bill of his cap hat showed that a size eight means twenty five inches around. That means Dad's head is more than two feet around. That's two subway sandwiches, enough to feed all six of us.

Mom buys two footlongs every time we go to Subway. She asks the Pakistani lady to cut twice so that we have three even pieces from each sandwich. That lady always acts like cutting the sandwich a second time is such an inconvenience. She knows that when my mom walks in, she is going to have to cut the sandwiches in threes, but she acts like she doesn't. Mom has to ask every time right before she tries to cut them in half.

I always grab the middle piece because it has the most meat. Nikki takes the other middle piece.

Mom gives Lil Man and Antoinette the ends. She and Dad take the ends too. Dad doesn't mind taking the end because he eats the last three bites Mikey can't fit in his stomach, as well as the bite that Antoinette doesn't finish. We call Dad the garbage disposal because he always eats what everybody else can't finish.

Everything looks small in Dad's hands, a sandwich, the steering wheel of the red car, and pens in his left hand look especially small because he curls his wrist around the pen and paper the way lefties do. I watch him write from the couch when he's doing math. He's taking a math class at the city college after work on Tuesdays. I look away when he lifts his eyes to look at me.

His backpack is small in his hands too, it's from Wal-Mart and doesn't have a brand name sewn onto it. It's blue and ugly. He doesn't care that it's ugly and small it was the cheapest one, and that's what matters to Dad.

THE PREACHER'S DAUGHTER

Everybody calls him Brian Johnson because there are two other Brian's in our class. There is Bryan Billups and Brian Nguyen. We call Bryan Billups "Bryan with a Y," and we call Brian Nguyen "Vietnamese Brian," but we always call Brian Johnson, Brian Johnson.

His favorite football team is the Minnesota Vikings, even though the rest of his family goes for the 49ers. He wears a Daunte Culpepper Jersey almost every day of the week. Every Monday he smells like sweat and dryer sheets. By Friday, he just smells musty. The number eleven on the back of his jersey is missing a one; he doesn't care though, and he always seems to get the girls despite his aroma on Fridays.

As Brian Johnson and I walk to the field behind his apartment to play catch, I ask him what he thinks about Kiana Rhodes.

"Kiana with the eyebrows? Hell Nah! Them

thangs look like caterpillars. And she dated e'rrybody in the eighth grade."

"Bruh, you dated her in sixth grade, and you was all over her."

"Yeah, that was before them eyebrows got all thick. Plus, she was the new girl, so you know I had to swoop first. I can't help that I'm a player!" I always ask him questions because I know his answers will make me laugh and because talking with him means that I don't have to play catch, I hate playing catch.

"If she plucked her eyebrows would you date 'er again?"

"I mean, maybe if she went to the barber and got a fade and a line up on them thangs, I might. But you know I can't get back with the same girl. I'm really tryna see what's poppin' wit Sherelle though!"

"Oh yeah, Sherelle is fine. She talkin' to Trey though."

"Maaan, you know Trey thirsty! His game is hella weak too. Ima pull her before eighth grade dance, watch. Yo, guess who asked me for your number though?" I look at him knowing he is going to tell me even if I don't guess. "Brenda!" he says with a huge grin. Brenda Okafor is the girl nobody can get with because her dad is a preacher, but everybody wants to be with her. She has flawless dark brown skin, and her clothes always look clean as if she pulls them out of the dryer every morning. Even her white Chuck Taylors stay white. She wears a gold anklet with a volleyball charm on it.

"Did you give 'er my number?"

"Hell yeah, you know I looked out for my boy. Good luck dealing with her pops though."
I smile at him then grab the football from his hands.

"Ima need more than luck. I might have to get baptized bruh." We both laugh.

MIKEY WALKS

We walk to school the long way every day. Mom doesn't let us walk the route that is ten minutes shorter, even when we are running late.

"Don't ever let me catch you walking down Story Road. Especially when you got your little brother witchu!" I don't mind it too much, except when it's raining or hot.

Mikey is the best kind of baby brother to have. He's like a little grown person. Dad calls him Lil Man; we all do. He is comfortable in his eight year old skin and he's the best listener I know. Every day on our way home from school I tell him about my day. He walks alongside me staring at the sidewalk in front of us as he chews on the yellow straw from the juice pouch he drank at recess hours before.

"Today in science, we were playing with all of Mr. Lowe's animals, and when it was time to clean up, this kid Richard put the snake back in the terrarium and accidently smashed the snake's head between the lid and the glass. I guess he was trying to rush back to his seat or something. There was blood all over the glass." Mikey's eyes widened and his mouth opened slightly with the yellow straw hanging loosely between his cheek and teeth.

"Yeah bruh, it was crazy. Mr. Lowe noticed when one of the girls screamed. He saw the blood then he went off! He turned so red he looked like the Kool Aid man." At this Lil Man grinned and shook his head.

"I ain't never seen a teacher that mad before he cussed at Richard and all of us sat down in our seats. It was dead silent. I wasn't scared because I didn't do it, but we didn't know what he was gonna do next. Next thing we know Mrs. Vasquez walks in and Mr. Lowe sends Richard to the office with her. Outside of that, the day was pretty slow, how about you?"

"My day was, good. I won at four square and Ashley gave me her brownie." He looked at me through the corners of his eyes to see how I'd respond.

"Uh oh Lil Man tryna be a mac daddy with the ladies?!" I grab him in a loose headlock and lightly grind my knuckles on his head. "I'm just messing with you, but make sure you focus on school, you'll have time for girls later ya hear me?"

"Yup."

COMMUNION

It looks like pieces of Oscar the grouch in a plastic bag. Qwaun and my other big cousin Ricky do it in silence. They look up really quickly when they see me emerge from behind the wall at the end of their court. I'm expecting them to say something to me but they don't. Something is different about today.

I always take the 71 bus from my house to the bus station at the mall and then walk from the mall to the wall at the end of their court.

I nod my head to say what's up, but I stay silent because I feel like that is what I am supposed to do. I sit on the yellow slide across from the park bench they're sitting on. Ricky has a brown stick in his hand that looks like the cinnamon sticks Granny uses to make candied yams on thanksgiving. Qwaun has the baggie with the pieces of Oscar the Grouch in it.

Ricky is so delicate with the cinnamon stick

14

between his fingers. He licks the side of it and starts to gently split it in half with his thumbs and forefingers. I know now that it can't be a cinnamon stick. He pours the contents of the stick out on the ground beside the bench. As if on cue, Qwaun opens the contents of the baggie and delicately pours it into the brown thing Ricky just split open.

We are silent.

I feel the same way I do at church on first Sunday when they pass the communion plates up and down the aisle, I don't really know what is happening but I know it's serious. The only difference between this and church is that something feels wrong about this.

So I stay silent.

Ricky rolls it all up till it looks like a cinnamon stick again. Ricky reaches toward Qwaun with it in his right hand, and Qwaun lights the tip of it with the purple lighter we used to burn ants this summer. It smells sweet at first, but then it smells strong and bad like when I went on a field trip to the farm in fourth grade, but worse.

On first Sundays, Mom never passes me the communion plate. She says, "Until you really know what it means you can't take it, not yet." Qwaun and Ricky don't pass it to me either, but they smile passing it to each other, kissing the cinnamon stick and looking up at smelly clouds.

TENNESSEE

"Get the fruit rolls from the fruit section. Those ones are made from real fruit and not just from candy like those other ones." The only time Mom ever lets us get anything from the grocery store is when we are going to drive down to Compton to see Aunty Rhonda, Uncle James, and my cousins. The trip down to Compton always starts the night before at Food 4 Less, where we buy "real" fruit roll ups, the purple ones that are stuck to plastic squares. We get seventy eight cent lunch meat packs and roman meal bread too. Mom fries a bunch of chicken that we put in the Styrofoam ice chest and eat cold on the road.

Mom loves taking trips, and so do we because we don't do it often.

My seat is in the back of the van next to the window, so I can stretch my legs out in front of the side door. Dad hates driving so he always rides shotgun. He calls himself the navigator even though Mom could get to Aunty Rhonda's house blindfolded. When we aren't all talking over each other, laughing, and repeating stories about other trips to Compton, the van is comfortably silent. Mom and I are always the only ones awake by the time we get to the grapevine on I-5.

"Mom?"

"What's up Kei-Kei?"

"How come we never visit Tennessee?" Mom waits a moment before she answers me. I see her eyes, which look just like mine, glance at me in the rearview mirror.

"Well, no one in the family is out there anymore, and I don't like the South Kei. Too many bad memories that I've spent years forgetting." Mom hesitates before she keeps talking. I look around the van and see everyone still sleeping. "When I was a little girl we used to shoot guns in the woods."

"You shot a gun before?" I ask with wide eyes.

"Yep. I started shooting guns when I was younger than you. We used to shoot at squirrels and bottles and cans. I loved being out in the woods. The leaves on the trees were greener than any green that you've ever seen. You could get lost out there in your imagination. We used to pretend to be pirates stranded on a deserted island trying to survive in the rainforest, or Native Americans living off the land. One time we were playing hide and seek and we couldn't find your Aunty Rhonda for hours. We knew we were going to get whooped when we got home. So we went home to get our flashlights to keep looking for her, and when we walked in, she was eating vanilla wafers on the couch and coloring in a coloring book. We were

17

upset and relieved at the same time." I smile as I stare at Mom's eyes in the rearview.

"Then one day when me and your Uncle Rick were out in the woods shooting at bottles and we smelled something foul." She gets quiet again; I stay silent in the backseat and just look at her eyes in the rearview mirror. She's staring at the road in front of her, but I can see tears welling up in her lower eyelid. I've only seen her cry at church and these 'almost tears' look different than her church tears.

"A Black man had been killed, and me and Uncle Ricky found his body out there in the woods behind our backyard. I was sick to my stomach. He looked like he'd been thrown into a shallow hole and the people who put him there didn't bother to bury him. We couldn't tell anybody or else whoever did it might have come after us. That's the way it is in the South Kei." We didn't say anything after that.

PAPA

Trey asked me why my dad always wore a Yankees hat. We sure as heck don't watch any baseball at our house, and if we do, we drive up to Oakland to see the A's play when Dad gets free tickets from his job. We only stay for four or five innings to eat junk food in the nosebleed seats.

I tell Trey what Dad always tells people when they ask about it: He's originally from Queens and he never liked the Met's so he wears the Yankee hat. Dad told me that when he was eight, Grandma Christine moved him, Uncle Kenny, and Aunty Michelle out here on his biological father's birthday. All she left was a note on the refrigerator saying that "she had had enough."

We visited queens once to see Abraham; that's Dad's biological father's name. Nikki was fifteen and I was ten at the time. She started calling him "GP" while we were there. Short for Grandpa, I guess. I didn't call him anything. I'd say, "hey," or "excuse me," if I needed something from him. I didn't call him "GP" because he isn't my grandpa, Papa's my grandpa.

Papa was my Dad's stepfather. I loved going to Grandma and Papa's house. He would always tell me not to open the green refrigerator in the garage. That's where he kept his "Papa sodas". I'd seen enough Budweiser commercials and beer at family parties to know what it was. I opened it once when he was napping and counted forty six red and white cans.

While Mikey and the girls were inside the house watching movies, I would sit in the garage and watch Papa work on his 1972 Chevy Nova. He and I never said much. He didn't smile very much either, but he'd put his big hand on my head as he walked in and out of the garage exchanging the wrong sized tool for the right sized one.

He kept the garage radio on all the time. Al Green was always playing. He moved slowly and he smelled like beer, the blue bottle of Aqua Velva he had in his bathroom, and his Rottweiler, Chleo. When the car wasn't all the way taken apart, he would drive Mikey and I to Burger King. He'd put Chleo in the back where there used to be a backseat, and he'd holler in the house and say, "Boys, C'mon we going to Kang Burga!" Mikey would sit on my lap in the front seat, and we'd ride wide eyed and smiling all the way. The inside of the car smelled like gasoline and was too loud for talking or the radio. Papa would drive fast down straight aways; we'd laugh and grip the torn vinyl seat that was stuck to my skinny legs.

The Nova always looked clean from the outside. I remember it being bright red one year, dark red the next, and turquoise was the last color I remember.

Papa died last year when I was twelve. He had bad lungs from smoking cigarettes. He must have smoked a lot of cigarettes before I was born because I don't remember ever seeing him smoke. I didn't cry when he died. I don't think he would have wanted me to. While he was lying there in his hospital bed, he looked at me with wet gray eyes, eyes that were usually behind gold framed glasses. He didn't say anything, and he didn't smile. I pulled the chair up next to his bed, and he put his big hand on my head as if we were still in the garage. Al Green had already sung all the sad songs we needed to hear.

I can still feel the breeze that rustles through the trees
And misty memories of days gone by
We could never see tomorrow, no one said a word about the
sorrow

PRINCESSES

Saturday is my favorite day of the week because I get to wake up, eat cereal, and watch Dragon Ball Z re-runs. Today wasn't one of those Saturdays, Mom woke us up by blaring gospel music all throughout the house. Gospel music means we will be cleaning until at least noon. I drag myself out of bed before Mom comes in with Dad's belt to *persuade* me and Mikey to get up. I slide off of the top bunk to the floor. I pull Mikey's covers off of him then I walk toward the door. I head into the bathroom and brush my teeth to the familiar cadence of Kirk Franklin's "Stomp"

"Keith, you and Mikey need to clean both bathrooms and your bedroom."

"Yes ma'am," I say through a mouth full of toothpaste.

"And when I say clean, I mean you need to wash your clothes and your bedsheets." Mom's voice trails off as she walks towards the backyard door.

"Yes ma'am," I repeat as I spit into the sink. I walk back into the bedroom to put on a t-shirt and slip on my sandals. Lil Man looks at me through I spoiled his entire day by pulling his blankets off.

"You can be mad at me if you want. I'm just tryna keep you from getting a whoopin' from Mom. We got the bathrooms today. I will do the toilets and shower if you sweep and do the sinks and counters." He nods his head and yawns. He knows I spared him from a guaranteed spanking.

I walk out of the room to go eat cereal before we get started. I pour out a bowl of what are supposed to resemble honeycombs and pull the milk from the back of the refrigerator. Nikki is in the kitchen washing the dishes and Antoinette is vacuuming the living room.

My sisters look like princesses from some African village. They're wearing scarves on their heads the way Mom, my grandmas, my aunties, and all my girl cousins do in the morning. Even though they're wearing basketball shorts and Dad's old t-shirts, they look like royalty every time they're in their scarves.

The women in my family are strong, but not the way TV and movies show black women; they don't have ridiculous attitudes and over the top personalities. They're just strong without apology.

Nikki hates losing at anything. Whether it's basketball or in the classroom, she always has to win. Little Antoinette doesn't take no for an answer. When she wants something she goes after it until she gets it. She told her third grade teacher Mr.

Lee that she was going to pass all the multiplying fractions levels on a computer game at her school. Mr. Lee made the mistake of telling her, "No, you won't learn that stuff until fourth grade." She stayed after school for two months straight in homework club and finished all of the levels that she said she would, and she passed the percentage levels too.

I chew my cereal and remember how Mom told us about being pregnant with Nikki when she was in college; she didn't finish until fifteen years later, but she finished.

BLACK SAMURAI

Mikey stayed at home sick and I didn't feel like walking home the long way, so I decided to walk home on Story Road instead. I am familiar enough with the street to know which side of the street to walk on and to keep my head down. I also know not to walk too fast and not to walk too slowly. The street looks different though. I am used to seeing it through a car window at thirty five miles per hour, but there's a lot that you miss when you're moving fast.

I see the familiar stuff like the brown and tan RV sitting on four flat tires in front of the pink house with the broken chain link fence. Across the street is the house with the poorly painted Virgin Mary on the slightly open garage door. I also notice things that would have been impossible to see through a moving car window. Through the fence in a backyard, I see a group of kids younger than Mikey sitting on a bench seat from an old car. I see mosquitoes flying around a puddle of rainwater on a wrinkled tarp that looks like it has been sitting in that driveway for a hundred years. I see handprints, initials, and cuss words etched into the concrete sidewalk squares as I stare at the ground in front of my feet. I also notice that I am noticed.

A dingy orange cat crawls suspiciously out from under an old Cutlass that is missing a hood. It tracks me carefully with its eyes as I walk. It stares at me as if to ask what I am doing there, walking down Story. The neighboring house has two Chihuahuas that bark at me from the living room window that faces the street. I begin feeling a bit uneasy as if all of these pets are letting the neighborhood know that my Mom told me not to walk home down Story. I'm still a good ten minutes from home, but I start walking a bit faster. I pull the headphones connected to my CD player in my hoodie pocket out. After putting them in my ears, I put my hood on and press play. The intro to Liquid Swords comes on. I mouth the words:

When I was little my father was famous, he was the greatest samurai in the empire…

Listening to the GZA or Wu-Tang makes me feel like I am a black samurai. It's audio courage. With each step I start nodding my head a bit more, and I begin rapping the lyrics:

…energy is felt once the cards are dealt
With the impact of roundhouse kicks from black belts…

After a while I forget all about the guard cats and dogs and cross over to the right side of the street because I need to turn up the next block. As I cross the street, I notice a couple of guys on bikes riding slowly behind me. All my Wu-tang courage leaves me just as fast as it came. I half jog-walk across the street and then return to a fast paced walk.

I can't look like I am worried, so I don't run. I stick my hand in my pocket and turn my CD player all the way down but keep my headphones in. I can't turn around and look at them a second time. I just have to act natural. I listen to them talking and laughing with each other. They're riding their bikes in the middle of the empty street now. I see the corner that I am going to turn on ahead of me. It's about half a football field away.

Their voices get louder until I hear them directly to my left; they're older than me, maybe 15 or 16. They're talking loud enough for me to hear. The one closest to me says, "Damn, I lost my CD player bruh." The one on the other side of him says, "For real? Damn that sucks you gotta get a new one." Then they both laugh. I know they are going to try and steal mine. I keep nodding my head, pretending to listen to music. I decide that once I get to the corner I am going to fake like I am going to cross the street and then run as fast as I can to the right, up the street.

Fifteen steps to the corner and with each step my heartbeat speeds up. Ten steps to the corner. They're so close to me now that I can hear the clicking of their bike chains. I stop nodding my head. Five steps to the corner. Through the side of my hood I see them stand up on their pedals, four steps, and I am nearly running. I reach the corner and fake one step off the curb and then break out into a sprint to my right. I look back and see that one of them took the bait. The other one turns up the street and is gaining on me. My street is only two blocks away but it feels like two miles.

The boy who "lost" his CD player catches up to me and turns into the driveway in front of me to cut me off. I try to push him as he jumps off his bike, but he is expecting it and shoves me down onto the sidewalk. I scramble to get up and try to push him again.

"Wassup lil nigga!" he yells as he approaches me. Just as I am about to stand to my feet he grabs the front of his white t-shirt and lifts it up. I see a silver pistol grip pressed against his brown skin, and I freeze.

"Yeah," he says, "calm yo' ass down." As much as I want to, I can't move; I'm stuck to the sidewalk like a fly on fly paper. "You got a CD player? Run that shit!" He says as he covers the gun back up with his long shirt. I still can't move; I'm not even breathing. I try to get my body to move but my arm won't listen to my brain. I hear the skid of a bike tire next to me, and I finally move when I turn my head to look at the other boy.

"Williams?" the boy who just showed up says my last name. My eyes are filled with water so I can't make out his face.

"You know this fool?" the boy with the gun says.

"Yo, that's Nikki's little brother, damn it." He rubs his head and punches his hand.

"Nikki on the varsity basketball team?"

"Yep."

"So what nigga, he won't say anything."

"Nah bruh, it's not a good look." The boy who knows Nikki walks over to where I'm sitting and looks me up and down as if he is thinking about what to say. I wipe my eyes before the tears fall out, and his face comes into focus. I don't know him personally, but I remember seeing him in the stands at my sister's basketball games.

"Get up!" my body listens to him and I stand to my feet. He takes a step toward me and leans in until his face is inches from mine. "If you tell anyone about this you gon catch a fade, you feel me?" I nod my head and put my headphones in my pocket. The boy who has the gun rolls his eyes in disappointment. The boy from the basketball games speaks again, "Aight then go home."

I nod and walk past him. The boy with gun steps in front of me so I can't pass. My heart starts racing even faster and my eyes swell with water again. He puts his hand on his shirt where the gun is hidden.

"You might catch more than a fade if you tell anyone about this shit, on everything." He stares at me through two piercing slits. I nod my head a third time and wait. Finally he moves out of the way to let me pass. I walk passed him and then start running the rest of the two blocks to my house. I cry silently and the tears stream along the side of my face.

JAYLEN

Jaylen is my best friend, and it has been that way since we were seven. We used to hang out behind the church when we were supposed to be at Sunday School. Jay would teach me everything I was supposed to know for any situation, like which of the church mothers to be nice to so they would give me peppermints from their purses, and which ones to avoid because they would make me grab them a fan or an envelope or a Kleenex. He also told me to always wear a belt just in case I got chased by the police, like his cousin Reggie who got caught because his pants kept slipping. He even showed me how to spit the right way.

Jay's mom Tisha is my play aunt and my mom is his. If I'm not at home cleaning on a Saturday you can always find me at Jay's house. He keeps a change of clothes at my house in the closet in a backpack, and I leave a backpack in his closet. Most of Jaylen's family stays up in Sobrante Park in

Oakland. He's the reason the Raiders are my favorite football team.

"Is your grandma making gumbo?"

"Yezzir, and banana pudding, plus the Raiders game is gon' be on too. Its days like this that I wish we still stayed up in Sobrante so we didn't have to take the train all the way up there."

"Real talk, your grandma's gumbo is enough of a reason to go up there every weekend. Yo Jay?"

"Yeah?"

"You ever wish your mom and pops stayed together?" He stops packing his overnight bag for our trip up to Oakland and sits down at the edge of his bed. He looks down at the floor for a bit, then stares past the closed door of his room. When he starts to speak, his voice is low as if he's thinking out loud.

"Nah. I seen that nigga put hands on my mom. That was the year we moved down here to San Jose. I was so small I couldn't do anything about it. That was the last time I saw him. I swear when I'm old enough I'm gonna beat the shit out of him the way he beat my mom." The look in his eyes is one I've never seen before. He looks focused and ready to act on his words if his father were to walk through the bedroom door right now.

"Yo, my bad bruh, I-"

"You couldn't know Keif, it's coo. Yo, toss me the controller to the Nintendo 64 though, because we gotta give my cousin Dante the business on Super Smash brothers." He blinks and his mouth twists into a familiar half smile. His left eyebrow has a small scar running through the middle of it

31

and it slants upward in the corner whenever he smiles.

After Aunty Tisha drops us off at the BART station in Fremont, we ask each other who we'd date the whole way up to Oakland.

"Aight Jay, Angela in *How Stella Got Her Groove Back* or Jada in *Set it Off?*"

"You know I gotta go with Jada. she's a rider in that movie and she's fine. Aight Sana in *Love and Basketball* or Stacy's lil sister in *The Wood?*"

"Sana Bruh," I say as I rub my hands together.

"For real? I woulda' went with Stacy's Sister."

"Nah, Sana is a hooper, and she got booty. Ok, Janet in Poetic Justice or the black girl on Clueless?"

"You already know Janet got that one!"

THE BOOK ROOM

Eighth grade students with a 3.0 GPA or higher can apply to be a teacher's aide as an elective. Most of the black students at East Hills Middle school sign up to be a Teachers Aid for Mrs. Turner. She is one of the few black staff members that works at our school.

Mrs. Turner works in the book room, where she organizes and catalogs all of the class sets of texts books and novels. Mrs. Turner is known for writing great recommendation letters for students who want to go to private high schools or competitive charter schools. I signed up to be Mrs. Turner's TA because Brenda Okafor signed up to be her TA, and the book room only has two TA's.

When I looked at the second trimester electives list in the quad at lunch, I tried my best not to smile from ear to ear. Brenda and I were selected as the fifth period TA's in the book room.

"Where you from?" I ask Brenda on our second day of working in the book room together.

"Where am I from? Or where is my family from?"

"Both."

"So is this an interrogation?"

"It's a question." I smile and put a text book on the shelf above me.

"It's two, actually." She smiles and puts a text book on the same shelf.

"Technically, you came up with the second one, and I'm guessing your fam' is Nigerian, Yoruba based on your last name."

"Ok Mr. Williams, are you the expert on the African continent?"

"Oh, so am I being interrogated now?" I laugh. She laughs and puts two books up on the shelf. I have to make a conscious effort to keep putting books on the shelf; if I don't, then I will catch myself staring at her. I could easily stop and watch her all day. Her movements are so graceful. I try not to be too obvious as I watch her slender arms moving from the book cart to the shelf and back again. Everything about her is perfect. She even smells good.

"Well I was born in San Francisco, and my daddy is Nigerian, my mom is black. She from Bayview."

"OK, so what brought you guys down here, besides the weather?"

"Honestly, the fog don't bother me. I prefer it, but my daddy is a software engineer during the week and a preacher on Sundays. He got a job with

Sundisk over in Milpitas, so we moved down here last year. Can you pass me that science book right there?" I hand her the book. "Thanks. My daddy brought a group from the church down here to start a small church." We finish sorting the entire cart of books. Mrs. Turner is gone delivering a class set of novels to a teacher.

Brenda turns towards me as I sit on the stool next to the bookshelf. I watch as her lips move and her cheeks are doing that thing that cheeks do when you're trying to hold back a smile. I smile when I see the dimple in her left cheek trying to hide with each word that she says. She's saying something about friends in San Francisco. Her dimple sneaks out again and I smile when I see it.

"What?" she asks, and I snap out of focusing on her dimple.

"Huh, what do you mean?"

"Why you smiling at me?"

"Oh uh, nothing. I just thought of something funny."

"Would you like to share?"

"Nah, it's really nothing." Silence, smiles, awkward laughs. She reaches out and lightly pats my chest.

"You are weird Keith Williams."

"'Cause I smiled?" I ask through a grin.

"It's a good weird Keith Williams." She walks past me towards the front of the book room.

BILLIE'S

Grandma Jean's seventieth birthday is coming up and the whole family is coming in from out of town to celebrate this weekend. Dad took the day off today and picked me and Mikey up from school. He made us do our homework in the backseat of the red car on our way to the barbershop.

"Can I go first?"

"Yeah Lil Man, just make sure you keep your head still. If you move and Macy messes up, then he'll have to cut you bald and you'll look like a milk dud at Grandma's party." We laugh as we get out of dad's red Nissan. I didn't mind going after Mikey, it gave me a chance to listen in on all the conversations and think about how I wanted my hair cut.

Billie's is the name of the barbershop, and I remember when I met Billie as a kid. She is an older lady who has silver hair that she wears in a short curly hairstyle. She's always happy. She always shouts "Where's my money Jack!" whenever she walks out from the back office. When I was about Mikey's age, I asked Dad who Jack was, he laughed and said, "Anybody who owes you some dough."

The inside of the barbershop never changes; it always has that familiar smell of the greenish blue liquid in the jars where all of the barbers keep their combs and scissors. The floor looks the same as the floor in the subway station in New York when we went to visit Queens. There are a bunch of tiny tiles, small white and black octagons. The old TV hanging on the wall in the corner is always playing sports news and occasionally draws the attention of everyone in the barbershop when they talk about a drug scandal or a major upset. There are five barber chairs. The one closest to the door is Hakeem's chair; he's an older guy with a receding hairline and coke bottle glasses. He's always yelling about how, "Bush done messed up this time!" The chair next to him has a new barber in it often, usually a young guy. The guy there today looks like he's only about seventeen. He's heavyset and has a baby face. He isn't cutting anybody's hair. He's sitting in his chair and talking in a low voice on the phone. The next chair is Mike Macy's chair everybody calls him Mace or Macy. Macy's bald and his clothes always look sharp. Creased button down shirt, pressed jeans and a fresh pair of Air Force Ones. He wears a gold hoop earring and has a fat wad of money that he keeps deep in his jeans pocket. He cuts our hair whenever we come in.

Next to him is Billie's son Dre. He's a little bit younger than Dad, and he looks like his Mom from the nose up. He's got the same cat like eyes and small nose with round nostrils. The last chair is Perry's. He's a really old man who has to be almost seven feet tall. He sits with his spider like daddy long legs crossed in his chair and watches sports news on the TV. Of all the times I've been to Billie's to get my haircut, I've never seen him give a single client a haircut.

Dad is always so smooth when he walks into the barbershop. He goes around and greets everyone with a fist bump or a handshake depending on if they have clippers in their hands. Mikey and me follow behind him and do the same.

"Wassup Keem?"

"Hey hey Big D," booms Hakeem's loud voice.

"What's good witchu young blood," Dad greets the kid on the phone. He gives Dad a fist bump and smiles.

"Hey Mace, how you livin?"

"I'm straight D. Good to see you and the boys. Man! Keith bout to be as tall as me." I try not to smile too big as I slap him five.

"Hey Dre, wassup?"

"Big D, long time no see," Dre says with a smile.

"I know it brotha. Hey Perry, how you doin' sir?"

"Well, I can't complain Derek. It's always a pleasure to see a father and his sons." Dad reaches out and shakes Perry's wrinkled hand. Perry's voice sounds like what I imagine Moses' voice sounded like, old and deep. It makes your chest vibrate when he speaks.

"Thank you sir," Dad says to Perry as he turns to Mace who is setting up his clippers at his station.

"Aight D, who's up first?"

"Lil man first, then Keith. Make 'im look good Mace. It's my mother in law's seventieth this weekend and all the family is coming together and throwing a party." Everyone chimes in with *wow's* and *that's wassup's*

"Aight D, I got you. Come on Mikey, let's hook you up with something special for your grandma."

I could spend hours in the barbershop listening to the conversations about politics, sports, and everything else in between. I listen intently to the stories about people I don't know who got caught cheating and now have to pay child support to their exes.

Perry tells us how his grandson graduated from Howard and is about to move back to the Bay Area to go to grad school at Stanford. Dre and the new guy, whose name is Adrian, get into a heated debate about the greatest NBA player of all time. Dre is arguing that no one could ever surpass Michael Jordan, and Adrian says that Kobe already has. It gets so heated that Billie comes out of the back office.

"Whoa Whoa Whoa!" she shouts and everyone falls silent. "Adrian, what I want to know is where's my money for that phone bill Jack?" Everyone bursts into laughter. "'Cause all your little phone calls is getting in the way of making this money boy. Please grab a broom and help me sweep up this floor." Adrian drops his head and smiles in embarrassment. He gets up and grabs a broom.

"Yes ma'am."

Just as everyone settles in from laughing Billie says, "And the greatest of all time was Dr. J." Everyone bursts into laughter again as Billie gives Perry a high five and walks back into her office.

THE MENDOZAS

Carlos' family is originally from Long Beach, CA. He said they moved up to San Jose because his great uncle who lived up here died and left the house to his dad. It's a nice house. It's the house on the corner, two houses down from ours. It has brown columns in the entrance and a stone walkway that leads up to the front door through the perfectly manicured grass. It is definitely the nicest house on the block. It even has a little house out in the back yard where Carlos's cousin Paulina and her 3 year old son Angel live in.

My dad and Carlos Senior are good friends because they're both into cars, and when my dad told him that we have family in Compton, Carlos Senior was excited to talk about LA. Carlos says that their house looks so nice because his tio who passed away was a contractor and did all the work himself.

Senior invited us over for a barbecue on Veterans Day. The Mendoza's parties were always a big thing. All of Carlos' family would come over until our entire block was lined with cars. One year, Senior invited his car club over on the 4th of July, and one of the neighbors called the cops because the cars were so loud. Senior kept asking the police officer, who was standing in his driveway, "Since when is it illegal to drive cars on the street?"

Today there is no car club and it's actually mellower than their parties usually are. Mom is helping Carlos's mom, Marta, bring out dishes from the kitchen to the tables in the garage. Dad is helping Senior fill the cooler with ice. They are laughing about something Senior said. Mikey and Antoinette are likely in the backyard jumping in the jumper with all of Carlos' little cousins. Nikki is talking to Paulina and some of Carlos' aunts at a table under the tree in the front yard. Carlos and I are playing basketball on the hoop that is set up in the street in front of the driveway.

"Dude how many cousins do you actually have?"

"Too many to count bro. I always ask girls if their last name is Mendoza or Ruelas because if it is, chances are we are related," Carlos says shaking his head.

"Ha, and you aint about that kissin' cousins life."

"Hell nah, we ain't no hill billies." We both laugh. Carlos puts up a shot that swishes through the net.

"You going out for the team this year 'Los?"

"Nah, I gotta focus on my grades. I got a D in Mrs. Stanley's class last year. That's why you didn't see me all summer, 'cause I was in summer school. Even my pops said I couldn't play this year." I catch his missed shot and flick up a quick layup. "My dad said, 'I don't want you to end up like your brother Lalo on probation or in jail.' The whole time he's yelling I'm thinking, 'man taking sports away is worse than probation.' Plus, ain't nobody tryna end up like *Lalo*. That foo is crazy. Love 'im, but he's crazy."

"How is Lalo anyway? I haven't seen that foo in years." Just as Carlos is about to answer, a maroon Chevy Impala comes roaring down the street blasting rap music. It screeches to a stop right across the street from the Mendoza house. Everyone's attention is on the car. One of Carlos's cousins even turned the music down.

"Uh Oh" Carlos says under his breath.

"Wassup? Who is that?" I ask Carlos who is holding the basketball and looking back and forth from his dad to the car.

"It's *pinche* Manuel, Paulina's baby daddy" I look over at Carlos Senior and watch him as he stands up from his game of dominoes. I look over at the passenger side of the car and a skinny Mexican guy gets out of the car and looks right over at Paulina, who puts Angel on her lap and is looking at her uncle Carlos. The skinny guy is wearing baggy pants, black Nike Cortez's with a red Nike check, and a wife beater tank top. He's covered in poorly done tattoos from the neck down.

"Yo Keith, be cool. Let's just sit on the curb."

We both sit down slowly. Paulina's baby's daddy is on some type of drugs. The smoke coming out of the car smells like the stuff Qwuan and Ricky smoked at the park. His eyes are all red and he's struggling to keep himself upright as he walks toward the house.

"I just want to see my son Carlos!" He slurs from the middle of the street. Carlos Senior gives Paulina a nod and a look that means she can go talk to him. My dad is watching Manuel as intently as Senior, so are all of Carlos' cousins and uncles who aren't laughing joking or eating any more.

Paulina walks over with Angel on her hip. All of the girls sitting at the table are giving Manuel dirty looks, and even my sister is eyeing him. Paulina stands on the sidewalk and Manuel approaches her. They start talking in low voices and Manuel kisses his son on the forehead. All of a sudden their conversation gets a bit louder. Paulina starts saying, "No Manuel, go home. You're faded." She puts Angel down, and he runs into the garage into Marta's arms. "Manuel you need to leave." Manuel reaches and grabs Paulina's left arm. She yanks it out of his grip, and before he could say another word, Carlos Senior bolts from the domino table to the sidewalk and is nose to nose with Manuel.

"'Lina, go inside," Senior says with squinting eyes locked on Manuel. She walks into the garage, grabs Angel, and disappears into the house.

"I can't see my son Carlos? Must be nice to have your family here!" He shouts as he points over towards me and Carlos.

"No, you can't see your son, and you got three

seconds to turn your ass around and get in that car before I put hands on you. The only reason I haven't already done it is 'cause I got my little nieces and nephews here, so take the opportunity while you still got it *puto. One-*"

"You ain't in Long Beach no more Carlos *estas en el norte vato*"

"Two-"

"You can't keep my son away from me forever. I love you Angelito!" Manuel shouts towards the house as he turns to walk back to the car. "You ain't gonna do shit Carlos. You ain't no OG. You know who calls the shots up here." He spits a loogie in the direction of Senior's '45 Chevy Truck. His saliva hits the shiny chrome bumper and dangles off.

Senior takes a step toward Manuel, grabs him by the shoulder and spins him around. He punches him square in the jaw. When Manuel's skinny body hits the street, Senior jumps right on top of him. Manuel is trying to block the punches with his hand, but Senior keeps hitting his head with punches like a jackhammer. Fist, face, concrete.

"Carlos *ya*!" rings Marta's sharp voice from the garage. Senior stops immediately, stands up, dusts off his short sleeve button down shirt with his left hand, and then kneels down to wipe the blood off of his right knuckles onto Manuel's shirt. The driver of the Impala stares at his friend's bloody face in shock. Senior stands up and looks at the driver of the car and points at Manuel.

"Get his ass outta here. And I don't ever wanna see your piece 'a shit car on my block again *ese*. When he comes to, let him know he talked to Lina for the last time, and if he wants to see his son again I'll send a picture to wherever he ends up getting locked up." Senior turns around and walks back to the domino table. He picks up where he left off as if nothing even happened.

READY

I stare at myself in the bathroom mirror, moving my eyebrows up and down, squinting my eyes, and smiling then not smiling and smiling again. I lean forward to look at my face closely; still no sign of hair on my chin, but the hair under my nose is getting darker, even though it's still soft like baby hair. I brush my eyebrows down with my forefingers and make sure all the hairs are laying down the right way. Then I take a step back from the counter and flex my stomach. I run my hand across my stomach and count all six abdominal muscles. The crunches I've been doing at night are really paying off. I flex my right bicep and feel the baseball shaped muscle with my left hand. The curls I've been doing with Dad's old weights in the garage have been working too. I take my wave cap off my head and lightly run my hands over the even waves on the top of my head. I grab my hard bristle brush from the counter and brush the sides and back of my head, then I brush the hairs under my nose. Jaylen told me that brushing it will help my mustache grow in faster.

"Keith hurry up! You not the only one who gotta get ready!" Nikki shouts through the bathroom door.

"Aight, I'm almost done," I say as she bangs on the door.

"I'm not playin'! Hurry up!" I roll my eyes and grab the Hugo Boss magazine advertisement from the cabinet under the sink. I unfold the flap where the scent sample is and rub the page on my chest and neck. Then I grab the deodorant and make sure I wipe at least four passes on each arm pit. Finally, I grab the baby powder from under the sink and put some in my underwear.

"Keith!" Nikki hollers.

"I'm done!" I grab my hard bristle brush and rush out of the bathroom to me and Mikey's bedroom at the end of the hall before Nikki can shout anything else at me.

I look at the floor where my outfit for today is neatly laid out. I pick up the freshly ironed black LRG t-shirt with the giraffe on it, the one I bought when I was with Jaylan and his cousins at the swap meet up in Oakland. I'm careful not to mess up my waves or get deodorant on it as I put it on. Then I put on the gray jeans that Mom bought for me when we went school shopping in August. Next, I put on my black socks to go with my black and white Allen Iverson Reebok's. I saved money all summer long to get them. Dad said if I could save up half he would pay the other half because there was no way he would pay one hundred dollars for a pair of shoes. I did yard work for Papa and cleaned both grandma's houses to save up that fifty. This will be the first time I wear them.

I've waited until midway through the second trimester to bust them out. I smell the new shoe smell in them before I put them on my feet. My foot slips right into them. They fit like a glove. I tie them up and know I am ready. Today, I'm going to ask Brenda to go the movies with me.

SHANNON

Shannon Lewis got suspended yesterday. She was wearing her hair natural. She had it parted down the middle with two afro puff pigtails in the back. A white girl asked if she could touch her hair, and Shannon said no. Later that day at lunch time, the white girl and a friend of hers walked up behind Shannon while she was eating. Each of them grabbed an afro puff, squeezed, and pulled. Shannon turned around and slapped the girl who had asked to touch her hair earlier. Shannon was taken to the office and they suspended her for three days.

Those white girls, who treated Shannon like a dog by petting her against her wishes, got no consequences for their actions, but Shannon got suspended. Sometimes I hate living in San Jose.

There aren't enough of us here, not on the North side at least. I want to move somewhere

where there are more Black people than everyone else at the school, so I won't have to deal with ridiculous situations like this.

I bet they didn't even ask Shannon what happened in class, the same way they didn't ask me what James Cox was doing in social studies class last year.

James kept writing my name next to the word Niger on the Africa map in the class set of textbooks. He was too stupid to know that it has a long "I" sound and a soft "G" sound, but I pushed all of his stuff off of his desk anyway. They took my Black butt to the office no questions asked and had me on detention for three days straight.

Shannon's parents, my parents, Brian Johnson's parents and I'm sure so many other Black mom's and dad's moved to the Northside to give us opportunities in this school district that others don't have. The same way their parents moved them out of the South to California in the 60's. But they don't know what it's like being thirteen nowadays. Black people lived in the same neighborhoods back then, so there schools had more than just the handful of black kids that are in my grade level. I know I should appreciate my mom and dad for putting us in good schools, but I'm angry that they did. Why couldn't we go to schools like Jaylan's cousins where I would be a part of the majority? I know nobody cares about those schools so they don't have nice stuff, but at least it would be *our* school. The North side makes me feel like I'm crazy, like I have split personalities. Sometimes I feel like I don't know who I am anymore. I hate that I like skateboarding and that I'm good at it because its "white." I hate that when I talk in class, the way I say stuff automatically changes to sound like everybody else. I say stuff like "totally," and "bro," stuff I'd never say around my family. I'm going to be myself from now on, and if they don't like it, they'll just have to suspend me like they did Shannon.

ICE CREAM

On cold nights, Dad loads us all up in the van and we head to Thrifty's. We are all smiles because we know we are about to get some ice cream.

"I want butter pecan," Antoinette declares.

"I want Vanilla and Chocolate," Mikey says with emphasis on the *and*.

"You can't get two flavors Lil Man," Nikki snaps back at him.

"Can I get two flavors Mom?"

"No, you have to decide which one you want more. The best flavor is Butter pecan though," Mom says.

"Heeey!" she and Antoinette say in unison as they high five each other.

"You know I'm getting chocolate, and I hope it has those little ice chunks in it. I love my ice cream hard as a rock," Dad says.

"Kei, what are you getting?" Nikki asks me.

"I don't know. Maybe chocolate or sherbet, depends how it looks through the glass."

"That sherbet is too sweet for me and it melts too fast," Dad says.

"Ooo, I want sherbet," Lil Man says.

We pull up to Thrifty's and pile out of the van. I exhale and see my breath in the night air. The bright red Thrifty's sign illuminates the smiles on my brother and sister's faces. Mikey and Antoinette rush to the automatic door and enter the store. As we walk over to the ice cream counter, I still can't decide what flavor I want. I look through the glass and the big tub of chocolate is brand new; it hasn't been touched. I don't even check the tub of sherbet.

The employee serving our ice cream is used to seeing us on cold nights and is generous with the scoops. I get chocolate, so does Dad. Mom and Antoinette get butter pecan, Nikki gets vanilla, and Mikey decides to get bubble gum. It's a new flavor and it's blue. Mom grabs a bunch of napkins and puts them in her jacket pocket. After dad pays we head back to the van.

THE MALL

"How much you wanna bet I can get her number? Twenty?" Brian Johnson asks me as we stare at the girl buying candy at the kiosk across from the Foot Locker.

"Nah Bruh, that's more than what I brought. You better make a bet with Carlos," I say as I push Carlos on the shoulder.

"Nah, I'm coo. I'm keepin' my money today, but she look Mexican Brian. She might not speak English, which means I could easily swoop the digits." He rubs his hands together and smiles at us. I pick up some cold fries from the McDonalds bag on the table and throw them in my mouth.

"Both of y'all trippin'. She look like she's a freshman or a sophomore. She's not gonna give you the time of day, and she taller than you Carlos," I say through a mouth full of fries. Brian Johnson and I laugh as Carlos gives me a blank stare.

"Age ain't nothing but a number my dude. Especially if you a young fly brotha like me," Brian Johnson says, dusting off his jeans and Minnesota Vikings Jersey.

"Height ain't nothing but a number either, especially when I can drop that Spanish game. You know Spanish is the language of love. Ima be like *¡Oye mamita!*" We all bust up laughing.

"Why you not trying to get at her Keith?" Carlos asks, and just as I'm about to answer, Brian Johnson speaks up.

"'Cause this fool is cup-caking over Brenda. They not even together and he acting all types of exclusive." He hugs himself, pretending to kiss a girl.

"I just told you she look like she in high school. I'm not sayin' I can't pull 'er, but it ain't worth it. Money says she already got a boyfriend." Just as I'm about to continue, the girl starts walking toward the direction of the food court where we are sitting.

"Yo, watch. Ima get that number." Carlos stands up and smooths the front of his t-shirt.

"Aight, go for it my dude. Don't come back empty handed." Brian encourages him and slaps him five. Carlos walks towards the Chinese restaurant that she's standing in line for. "Carlos is 'bout to get curved bruh." We both laugh. "But foreal, how's it going with you and Brenda?" Brian asks as we both keep an eye on Carlos.

"Bruh, she's so cool. I swear, I can talk to her non-stop, that's all we do in Mrs. Turner's while we sort books. I just don't know where to go next, you feel me?"

"Whatchu mean, like ask her to be yo girl?"

"Yeah man I dunno, it's like she's a cool friend, and if we were to get together and then break up, I would hate to lose her as a friend."

"Dang bro, that sound serious. It sounds like you all up in your feelings! I feel whatchu saying though." Just as I'm about to speak I notice a tall skinny white dude eyeing Carlos from across the food court. The girl keeps glancing over at the other guy but continues the conversation with Carlos.

"Bruh, you see dude across the way eyeing Carlos. This chick is tryna get our boy caught up," I say as I point to the tall guy.

"Oh yeah. Man, she tryna get our boy beat up let's chill for a minute." We wait a little while, and then the guy starts walking over towards the Chinese restaurant.

"Aight Keith, let's go." We walk in the same direction and get to Carlos at the same time as the tall guy does. He stands between the girl and the three of us.

"You talkin' to my girl?"

"Looked like yo' girl was talkin' to me bro." Carlos steps forward as he responds and stares the guy dead in the eye.

"Yo, 'Los, let's dip out of here. This foo ain't worth it," I say as I put my hand on Carlos's shoulder.

"You better listen to your little friends and get out of here before you end up hurt," the tall guy says with his eyes locked on Carlos. Brian Johnson steps up to the guy.

"Woah there buddy. It looks like you are outnumbered three to one. Don't get it twisted, you will catch a beat down if we think it's worth it. I suggest you check yo' girl walking around here thirst trapping fools. We all saw she was nothing but smiles and conversation a couple minutes ago." The tall guy takes a little step back. I notice a mall security guard walking toward us.

"Hey, rent-a-cop coming our way, let's roll," I say, and the guy backs up even more. As we head toward the mall exit, Carlos stops and turns back toward the tall guy and the girl.

"Yo, when you tryna holler at a real one, holler at me Maritza. Yeah she took my number down bro, just FYI." He turns back around and keeps walking. We all laugh and slap Carlos five.

TACO BELL

"You sure she's asleep?"

"Yeah Keif, stop trippin'. I do this all the time." I can hear Jaylen quietly slip out of his bed and walk over to his bedroom window. I get up from the floor where I was pretending to sleep and tiptoe to the window. The only light in the room is the orange street light shining in from the parking lot outside. He silently slides the window open and carefully pops the screen out and sets it on the floor under the window.

'Aight Keif, you go first. Just climb down that pole going down the side of the building." I stick my head out and look to the right. There is a pole there that looks sturdy enough to hold my weight. "Hurry up bruh, just go." I slip out of the window and grab the pole with my left hand and then with my right. It's easy to slide down. Once I hit the ground I look up and find Jaylen sliding effortlessly down it too.

He grabs an old broomstick and uses it to slide the window closed, making sure to leave enough space to open it when we get back. He puts the broomstick down and walks quickly between the wall and some bushes until we come out on the other side of his apartment building where all the residents' cars are parked.

"Bruh, I was trippin'. I thought for sure we were gonna get caught."

"Nah, I told you I do this all the time. My mama sleeps like a rock, and Isaiah won't snitch as long as we bring him something back."

"Where do you be going when you sneak out?"

"I walked all the way to Keisha's house one time, and she didn't even let me in bruh. I was upset. She came outside though and we chopped it up for a good minute. She told me her pops asked her if she wanted to move with him to Pittsburgh."

"I thought you and Keisha was done. Y'all are worse than a married couple." We both laugh.

"We are done with relationships, but that's my homey. I always got love for her." We walk out to the street and cross in the direction of the Taco Bell with the bright red neon sign that says "Open 24 HRS"

"Is she gonna move with her dad?"

"I told her to do what's best. I obviously want her to stay, but she said her mom's new boyfriend be trying to act like her daddy and she hates being there."

"Yeah, that sounds like a wack situation." We walk into Taco Bell and order more tacos than we are actually going to eat. The moment we walk out of the restaurant, a police car skids into the parking lot. The cop who is driving comes out of his car with his gun drawn; he points it right at us.

"Get down on the ground!" I drop the bag of tacos on the ground and lay down on the sidewalk. I look to the left and see Jaylan's face. He is just as scared as I am. The passenger side door of the police car opens up and I see a set of shiny black boots walking in our direction. The cop who was driving walks towards me. I close my eyes, afraid of what is about to happen next.

"Put your hands behind your back, now!" I listen immediately, then I feel the worst pain I've ever felt. There's a sharp pain in my spine and I feel the weight of the police officer on my back. All of the air is pushed out of my lungs. I can't even yell out for help.

"Stop, you're hurting him!" I hear Jaylen scream. I look over at him and the other cop is putting a plastic zip tie around his wrists.

"Shut up and move over to the curb," the other cop says to Jaylen as he drags him over to the curb. The officer on top of me zip ties my hands and drags me to the curb too. I sit up and scoot next Jaylen.

"We didn't do nothing." I cough as I catch my breath. The cop who was driving towers over us with his hand on his gun, which is in the holster now. He doesn't respond. He leans his head to his right shoulder and listens to something that I can't make out on his radio.

"Why y'all sweatin' us? We ain't do nothing," Jaylen shouts at the officer.

"Shut the hell up and wait, or I swear to God I will put you down." Comes the voice of the other officer behind us.

Put us down?

"Grab their ID's," the officer in front of us says.

"We don't have any ID's, We only thirteen," Jaylen says. The cop behind him gives him a swift kick to the back with the side of his foot. "I said shut the hell up. You don't speak unless you're spoken to." I start crying as I see the look of pain on my friend's face. He starts crying too. The officer lifts us up to our feet and grabs our wallets out of our back pockets then pushes us back down on the ground. I glance back and see the picture I keep of my Papa fall to the ground and the movie ticket stub from when Brenda and I went to the movies.

"Please, just let us go home," I say through tears. They ignore me. Jaylen is next to me trying to control his breathing between muffled sobs.

"Jaylan Thompson and Keith Williams." We look up and see the cop who was driving holding our student ID cards. "What the hell are you doing out here? Selling drugs? Were you about to rob this place?"

"No! We j-just bought food," I say trying to stop the tears from falling.

"We live in Sandalwood, across the street!" Jay says.

"Don't raise your voice at me boy," the cop says and then is interrupted again by the static voice on the other side of the radio. He nods to the other cop.

"Cut 'em loose. We gotta head over to Snell and Capitol." The other cop cuts the zip ties off of our wrists and stands us up. The cop who was driving throws our wallets on the ground in front of us. "Your asses shouldn't be out at one o'clock in the morning. I suggest you go the hell home and stay there."

Both cops get in the car and speed away with their lights flashing and siren blaring. We stand there silent for a moment. Then Jaylen lets out a yell in the direction of where the cops are heading. He pushes over the trash can outside of the taco bell entrance and starts kicking it. I rush to him and wrap my arms around him from behind. He tries to fight his way out, but I interlock my fingers and squeeze harder. I pull him away from the trash can until we both slump onto the sidewalk and cry with our arms around each other's shoulders.

13 AND SOME CHANGE

Ricky is fifteen and he's the best basketball player on his team at Milpitas High School. Uncle Rick says that if he keeps his grades up he'll be able to get a scholarship in two years when he graduates. Ricky loves going to Flickinger Park and playing for hours.

Sometimes I ride my bike to the park to watch him play. He always asks, "You playing today?" I always say no, but today is different. I say yes because I really feel like I'm ready.

I've been playing with Ricky at his house more often, and me and Carlos have been playing one on one every day after school. Plus, I've been doing toe raises to get my hops up. Even though I'm at least two years younger than everybody else at the park, I feel confident I can take them. I've watched these guys so much, that I know everybody's bad habits. I tie up my Nikes and walk onto the cement court with Ricky.

"Aight, it's me and my lil cuz Kei'. We will take three more folks on our team so we can run fives." Three more guys walk over to where me and Ricky are standing. The tallest guy to join our team is Chris, who plays on the varsity team at Nikki's high school. The other two are Roderick and Kenny. They play at Ricky's school on the junior varsity team.

The five guys on the other team are a mix of regulars at Flickinger. The shortest one on their team is the best player. His name is Anthony; he's quick and has a jumper. The other four guys are decent, and they're used to playing with each other.

"You really gonna play with little man on your team?" Anthony, the short point guard, asks Ricky as he dribbles toward the half court line. *Lil man? I'm darn near as tall as you!* I think to myself.

"Yep, and we still gon' run y'all. Shoot for take out," Ricky says, nodding towards the basket. Anthony shoots and swishes the shot from well behind the three point line. Ricky has a habit of wiping the bottom of his shoes in between plays. I do the same thing at the start of the game.

"Aight, our ball. Check up from half court." Ricky checks Anthony the ball as the rest of us match up with guys who are close to our height. For me, that's the next smallest guy on their team; he's a light skinned guy with red shorts and a black Nike tee shirt.

The game gets going faster than I expect it to. The guy I'm covering scores the first point of the game. He blew right past me. I could tell this was going to be harder than I thought it would be. Its one thing to watch my cousin play with these guys, and it's another thing to actually run with them.

On offense, I set up on the left wing just outside of the three point line. I wait for a screen to block my defensive man as Ricky brings the ball past half court. Chris, the tall guy on our team, pops out of the key and sets up a screen for me so I can cut towards the hoop. The guy in the Nike shirt gets hung up on Chris, and Ricky sees that I am open under the hoop. He fires a rocket of a pass inside to me. I'm surprised at how hard it was and more surprised that I caught it. I dribble once then turn to put up an easy layup. I score the first point for our team. I hustle back down to get on defense and Ricky gives me a high five as the other team brings the ball up.

The trash talking starts, and I just listen. I'm the youngest one here; the last thing I need is for them to think that I'm making fun of them. They're way bigger and stronger than me.

"Go ahead and shoot from way out there. I'll give you that every time. You not gon' make it… See you ain't got a jumper like that."

———————

"Don't get your ankles broke out here bruh."

"Please, only ankles you breakin' is your own doing all that dribbling. Put up a shot already."

"And one! How you gonna hack me every time I drive to the basket?! I know you can't guard me bruh, but stop hackin'."

"No blood. No foul."

"This ain't no prison ball. You better go somewhere with that nonsense."

"Seven, four us. Y'all plan on scoring anymore?"

"We playing to eleven and win buy two, so don't get too excited."

"Tied, seven up. You done got real quiet. You mad?"

"Hurry and check the ball up. Ain't nobody tryna talk. Let's actually play the game."

"Oh, you was doing a whole lotta talkin' three points ago."

The score is ten, eleven with us in the lead, and I end up with the ball. I'm exhausted, but I don't want to let Ricky down. I have to prove to these guys that I'm not just a little kid anymore. I really have to prove it to myself.

I'm at the top of the key, and I can see where everybody on my team is. I wait for them to get some good off the ball movement. Just as Nike t-shirt steps up to defend me, I see big Chris set a screen for Ricky. Ricky cuts towards the basket and jumps. I throw up an alley oop pass and I watch it in slow motion. The ball rotates as it lobs toward Ricky's hands. He grabs it out of the air and slams it into the hoop.

"Game," Ricky says, still hanging from the rim. He drops down and starts high fiving everybody. I high five everyone too. The point guard on the other team approaches me.

"How old are you? 'Bout thirteen and some change?" The little point guard asks.

"Yup," I say as I nod my head and give him a fist bump.

"You got heart bruh. Keep running with us and you'll be ready to play varsity as a freshman next year." I try not to smile too big, but I can't hold it back when I catch eyes with my cousin who is smiling and nodding his head at me.

XIOMARA

"You gotta help me decide what to get Brian Johnson for his birthday," Xiomara tells me as she colors in the 'W' on our Westward Expansion poster.

"Foreal? 'Mara you gotta be kidding me," I say as I laugh and pick up a blue marker to color the 'X' on the poster.

"Sshh! Damn Keith, you hella loud. Don't be putting me on blast like that." She lowers her head and keeps coloring. I glance over at Mr. Lin, our history teacher. He's calmly flipping through a textbook with his feet up on his desk the way he usually does when we work on group projects.

"Nobody is trippin' off you girl, chill."

"I just don't want Leslie over there to hear because she's friends with Sherelle, and you know she's gonna run to her and tell her to cuff Brian before I swoop on him." She's whispering and cutting her eyes left and right.

"You acting crazy right now, drawing all types of attention to yourself." I start tracing the outline of the covered wagon underneath the word "Expansion" on the poster. "Yo, off topic, but why we gotta learn about white people getting sick as they travel to California though?"

"Ok Keith, now you're just avoiding the question. I'm asking you for real for real. Give me something, favorite color, clothes brand, something." She drops the marker on the table and crosses her arms as she leans back in her chair.

"Xiomara, I've known you since fourth grade, Brian too, and you've been crushing on him since probably before I moved to this side of town. My question is why? I mean, he's my boy and all, but you and I both know that he's a player. And not a very good one either."

She looks at me and pouts her lip out trying to hold back a smile. "I know Keith, I Know! It's just, I don't know, he's cute and funny, and maybe I'm the one that will change his player ways." I stop drawing to look up at her. We both bust up laughing at the same time. "I know I sound crazy right now, but I can't help it." She grabs a marker and leans in to color another letter. "You know what I'm talking about Kei. It's that burning in your stomach. I know that's how you feel about Brenda," she says in a whisper. I look around the room to see if anyone heard her. I look back at her and she's smiling.,

"Yeah, Brenda's not a player though," I whisper back.

"You don't know that. She might just be really good at it. She prolly got a choir boy at church singing some slow jams to her every Sunday." We both crack up again. We quickly stop and get ourselves together before Mr. Lin looks at us.

I lean in towards her. "Ima draw you as the daughter dying of dysentery hanging off the back of this wagon if you keep acting up," I whisper as I point at the drawing of the wagon. She holds back another laugh.

"First of all, my beautiful brown self would be somewhere in Mexico talking to the Aztec gods, not on a wagon going to *pinche* Oregon. Second of all, please Keith, what should I get him? And don't tell me a freaking Vikings shirt. A regular chick like *Sherelle* would get that for him," she says as she rolls her eyes and flicks her hair back behind her shoulder.

"Ok, just 'cause you my homie, Ima help you out." She sits up and smiles with wide eyes. "If you're gonna get him food, he loves Togo's Meatball sandwiches with extra banana peppers."

"Kei', what am I gonna look like giving him a sandwich?" She throws her arms up and squints at me.

"I'm giving you gold here girl! That's personal stuff. Sherrelle don't know this fool's weird cravings. If you don't want my advice I can--"

"No No, sorry Kei', go ahead!"

"Ok, he also likes Nike socks. I mean he *really* likes them. He sleeps in them and washes them

71

only on Tuesdays. He swears that they make him better at football. "

"Keith, your friend is so weird."

"I know. He wears that same jersey every day, and he has weird attachments to stuff, but that's my boy."

"That's why I like him though; he's so unique. We would be the power couple at East Hills Middle School if he only stopped wasting his time with *Sherrelle* and realized that he got a real woman in me!" We both laugh again.

"Keith and Xiomara!"

"Sorry Mr. Lin," we respond in unison.

CORNER STORE

"Kei', are you done with your homework?"

"Yes sir."

"Here, take this and walk to the corner store and get a half gallon of milk and some bread. You can get you some chips or whatever with the change." My dad hands me a folded ten dollar bill.

"Ok," I say as I grab the ten out of his hand and then lean forward to put my shoes on. Dad disappears down the hallway to his bedroom. I turn off the TV and head for my room. I grab my backpack, a bag of sunflower seeds, and my house key before heading out the door. The corner store is only a couple blocks away, and being able to buy something with Dad's change makes being the one who always has to walk to the corner store a good deal.

As I head towards the corner I see Carlos shooting hoops. I walk out into the street to say what's up before going to the store.

"Wassup Keith, you wanna play?" Carlos says between heavy breaths.

"Wassup 'Los? Nah man, I gotta go grab some stuff from the corner store." I spit out a couple of sunflower seed shells and give him a fist bump.

"Let me roll witchu. I wanna get me a Gatorade."

"Fosho." Carlos runs into his open garage and then into the house. Not a minute later he comes running back out counting some crumpled dollar bills.

"You have Mr. Gonzalez for P.E. right?" Carlos asks as he smooths out the last crumpled dollar in his hand.

"Yeah, that fool's crazy. Are y'all doing cross country right now?" I throw some more seeds in my mouth.

"Yeah! Yesterday he had us running like we were going to the Olympics or something! I hate that fool. I was like a zombie in my next class; plus, I forgot my deodorant that day, so I had the whole classroom smelling all funky!" Carlos waved his hands in front of his nose and shook his head.

"That's disgusting." I laugh as I spit some seed shells into the street. "Yeah, I just keep it mellow when we are running the mile. He's always like 'Williams, I know you got a lot of potential, push yourself buddy push!' You know how he always be calling people buddy."

"I know right, super creepy." Carlos laughs.

We walk into the corner store and nod at Mr. Singh.

"Hello boys, how are you today?"

"Good Mr. Singh, thanks," I say as I head toward the refrigerated section in the back of the store.

"Fine thanks," Carlos says as he heads towards the chips aisle. I grab a half gallon of 2% milk and head toward the bread aisle to get a loaf of roman meal bread. I place both items on the checkout counter then head to the slushee machine. I grab a cup and a dome lid, mix the tropical pineapple flavor with the blue raspberry flavor, then head back to the counter. Carlos is paying for a red Gatorade and a bag of Funions. I pay for my stuff, throw it in my backpack, then we head out.

"On some real stuff though Carlos, do your parents ever fight?"

"All the time bro. Why you think I'm always outside playing basketball or at your house? They go at it about who spent what and about how my dad is always with his car club."

"Yeah, my folks went in last weekend. I heard 'em yelling through the wall."

"Your parents seem like the Cosby's. I can't even imagine them fighting. What was it about?" he asked as he twisted the top on his Gatorade and took a long drink.

"I couldn't really tell. My mom kept saying something like 'you never listen,' and my dad kept yelling over her like 'what do you want from me Cynthia what?' But like, he wasn't really asking to get an answer." Carlos reaches out to hand me

75

some Funions, but I shake head and sip on my slushee.

"Sounds serious. How did it end?" Carlos asks through a mouthful of Funions.

"My pops left the house and came back later that night. My mom stayed in the room."

"Where do you think he went?"

"He went to my Uncle Rick's house. My cousin Qwaun called me up asking what was up because my pops and Uncle Rick were out in the car talkin' for a long time."

"It sounds like they'll be cool bro. I wouldn't worry."

"Yeah, I feel you. It's just I don't remember them ever going at it like that before. And today is the first day that they've talked since then."

"You worried?"

I pause and think before I answer. The truth is I am beyond worried; I'm terrified. Most of my closest friends, except for Carlos, only have one parent at home. I don't want to be another one of those black boys only seeing my daddy on weekends or worse, never seeing him at all. I look up at Carlos.

"Nah, I'm not trippin'."

CHRISTMAS

"You're gonna roll with me this year for the Angel Tree deliveries. I want you to see that you always got something to appreciate." That's what my dad told me last Friday when I was playing video games in the living room. Every year my dad volunteers to deliver presents to the children of inmates in San Quentin. Our church does a toy drive and makes bags for the families that sign up.

I look out the window of the passenger seat of the Minivan and see the yellow streetlights passing. Tonight is cold, so I've got a sweater and a jacket on. I even wore my blue and gold Warriors beanie that Nikki bought me for my last birthday. I glance in the back of the van to look at all of the black garbage bags filled with presents. They have green papers attached to them with last names and numbers written on them. Wright-3, Lawson-2, Hernandez-6 Kempton-7, De La Vega-2, Jackson-2, and a bunch more buried under those ones.

"How many of them are we gonna deliver Dad?"

"There are eighteen back there, and there are fifteen other guys from church delivering about the same amount of bags. What's the math on how many bags that is?"

I close my eyes and do some quick mental math. "It's about three hundred bags."

"Yep, and that's only inmates who heard about the program, but there's tons more who are locked up and have kids." We turn onto a street that is lined with old apartment buildings. There are dumpsters on the street with trash littered around them. All the cars we are passing are older and beat up with the exception of a Mercedes Benz with huge shiny rims on it.

"Dad, why'd you bring your folding knife with you?"

"As you can see, we gotta go to some rough neighborhoods. Don't worry though son, I've never had to use it. When people see all 6'5" 260 pounds of me, they don't give me any problems." He pulls up to an apartment building and pulls the handbrake. He turns on the dome light and looks at a clip board.

"Aight son climb in back and grab the bag that says Gannon-4 on it." I climb in the back and shuffle some bags around. I find the Gannon bag and pull it out from under two other bags.

"Got it!"

"Let's go then." Dad opens up his door and walks around to the sliding door; he opens it and I hop out with the bag in my hand. My dad grabs the bag and we head toward one of the old apartment buildings. "I don't want you to say anything at all when we get up there. You look at what I'm doing and do the same thing. If I'm not smiling then you not smiling. Got it?"

"Yes sir," I say as I follow my dad up a flight of stairs to a second floor apartment. He knocks on a door that has a rusted old number seven on it.

"Who is it?!" we hear a man's voice shout from the other side.

"Angel Tree delivery," My dad says back in a deep voice.

"Angel who?!" The man's voice sounds annoyed on the other side.

"I'm here to deliver some Christmas presents for the kids." I hear what sounds like a tiny gasp and then I hear tiny footsteps running towards the front door. Dad and I both have our ears turned toward the door to hear what is going on inside. The next thing I hear is a loud smacking sound and a thump on a wall. I jump because I'm startled by the loud sound. I hear a toddler crying on the other side.

"Getcho ass in the room and stop crying!" The same voice shouts on the other side of the door. I look up at my dad, and I can see his jaw flexing as he clenches his teeth. I hear locks turning on the other side of the door. The door swings open and there's a shirtless man wearing jeans that are sagging to about his thighs. He's got blue boxers on and dirty socks. He has a du rag on and braids underneath. He looks mixed, light skinned with light eyes and patches of beard on his cheeks.

"Wassup Nigga?" he says to my dad with a mean mug on his face. I'm shocked at my dad's response.

"Hi, I'm here to deliver some Christmas presents to the four children of Marcus Gannon. Would you like to sign for them?" My dad could easily break this guy in half if he wanted to, but he's standing there holding a clipboard out calm and cool. The guy at the door squints at the clipboard as if my dad is holding moldy food. I glance inside and see a kid no older than two standing in the hallway in a diaper that looks full. He has fresh tears on his face and snot running down his lips.

"They ain't my bitch ass kids." He turns around to walk away from my dad. "Shaneel, come talk to this nigga at the door!" he shouts. The baby who was standing in the hall turns and runs into the room off the hall. Out of the same room, a girl in a yellow robe that is only covering the top of her thighs and is barely covering her chest walks out. Her eyes are red and she keeps pulling hair onto her face as she walks. "Hi, can I help you?" she asks as she tightens her robe and fidgets with the collar. My dad extends the clipboard toward her and says the same thing.

"Hi, I'm here to deliver some Christmas presents to the four children of Marcus Gannon. Would you like to sign for them?" The woman glances down at me and the bag and fidgets with the collar some more.

"Oh my god, Marcus sent these? H-he's out?"

"No, he's not," My dad says with the clipboard outstretched.

"Oh, how is he?" Are y'all related, or have you seen him?" I look down and see that the baby has snuck out of the room and is watching the conversations from his mom's calf.

"I don't know him personally ma'am, but there is a letter in the bag from him, so please sign and I will be on my way."

"Ok." She grabs the pen and signs the clipboard. "Thank you."

"God bless, Merry Christmas," My dad says as we walk downstairs towards the van.

As we drive to the next house I think about what I just saw.

"Dad, why didn't you get mad at that guy?"

"Kei, this world is full of broke down people. Those people back there were on drugs. I felt bad for them more than anything else. If I had a house big enough, I woulda taken all of them kids up outta that house, 'cause the kids are the ones that really suffer. Whipping that dude's tail wouldn't have solved anything, but prayin' for him will. That skinny dude was able to see two real men standing at his door tonight delivering presents, and so did

81

that young girl. So hopefully she don't continue the cycle of getting with busters who are gonna use and abuse her. You follow what I'm saying?"

"Yes sir."

"UNOFFICIALLY OFFICIAL"

"You ever been back to Nigeria with your family?" I ask as Brenda puts her pink backpack down on the table in the library. We sit down across from each other.

"Yeah, we went back when I was eleven for one of my dad's cousin's weddings."

"That's dope. I want to go out of the country. Maybe y'all can take me with you next time." Brenda looks up from her open backpack and smiles.

"Yeah, I will just pack you in my suitcase. I'll make sure to throw some snacks in there and some water. It's a long flight."

"Coo, I can't wait." We catch eyes and laugh and then just stare at each other. Staring at each other used to be awkward; it's not any more. It's like spaces between paragraphs, that white space on the page that doesn't say anything but means so much. "So what is it like, Nigeria?"

"Like, the food? The people?"

"Just the whole experience, what was it like?"

"I love everything about it. We spent most of our time in Lagos. It's a major city, kinda like a San Francisco or New York. We also went to my dad's village where I met a bunch of my dad's family for the first time. I just felt at home," she said as she leaned forward to rest her forearms on the table.

"Would you ever move there?" I ask. She squints and looks out the window.

"Maybe. When I'm there it's like the 'me' part of me feels at home. Everybody looks like me, you know? Like all the rich people are Black like me. I'm talkin' doctors, lawyers, actors, everybody." She closes her eyes but keeps her head in the direction of the window. "And even the poor people look like me. It's like I didn't have to think about what others thought about me." She opens her eyes and turns to look at me. "Here in San Jose, I'm always thinking about how others are looking at me, especially when most of the people I'm around don't look like me, like my teachers, doctors, and even my friends. I don't know. I feel like I'm not making sense." She sighs and gives me a half smile.

"Nah, I hear what you're saying completely. It's like you always have to kinda adjust for everybody around you."

"Yeah, exactly. In Nigeria there was none of that, no adjusting. I had my hair in braids and so did a bunch of other girls. There were girls with straight hair too, but it was cool seeing a bunch of natural hairstyles."

"That's wassup. I seriously gotta visit at some point in my life." I open my backpack and pull out my Math textbook. "We should probably get to work. What time you gotta be home?"

"What time is it now?" she asks. I look over at the clock hanging above the librarian counter.

"It's about 1:15."

"Oh, I got a ton of time. I don't have to be home until four o'clock. What about you?"

"I told my pops I would be home about the same time. What did you tell your folks you were doing?" I ask as I open up to a clean sheet of paper in my notebook.

"What do you mean?" she asks as she crosses her arms and raises an eyebrow.

"I mean, did you tell them you were doing homework with a handsome young brotha like me?" I rub my hands together and smile at her.

"Wow." Brenda laughs and shakes her head. "Boy, you are crazy. What did you tell your folks?"

"I mean, I told them that I was doing homework at the library with Brenda."

"And I told mine I would be here with you. My dad is a preacher not a prison warden." My head drops and I smile, speechless. "We aren't on a date, are we Mr. Williams?" She reaches across the table and lifts my chin with her finger. I look at her raised eyebrows and her smile.

"Nah, Miss Okafor. We just doing homework." She nods her head and pulls out her notebook. I lean forward to speak then sit back in my chair. I lean forward again and rest on my elbows. "Could you see yourself dating me Miss Okafor?" I almost can't believe it came out of my mouth. Brenda is trying to purse her lips together to hold back a smile.

"Are you asking me to be your girlfriend, *Mr. Williams?*" she asks as she leans forward and stares into my eyes.

"Yeah," I say without taking my eyes off of hers.

"Well, to answer your first question, yes, I can see myself dating you. But my parents won't allow me to have a boyfriend until I turn sixteen." I start to nod my head slowly, and my shoulders drop a bit. "To be one hundred with you Keith, I thought a lot about just doing it without them knowing. I like you a lot, but I respect what they want, and I like being able to tell them stuff like me and you are doing homework together. My older sister is messing around with some dude from church and it's a mess. She always lying about stuff. I just wanna do things different than her." She drops her head and looks at her notebook. She scribbles some circles in the margin of a blank page. "You mad?"

"Mad? Nah, not at all. I can respect that. I mean, it makes sense." I smile at her. "Honestly, I didn't want to jack up our friendship. Like if we had gotten together then broken up or something, I would be more upset that I lost a friend you know?"

"You planning to break up already?" she asks and we both laugh.

"Nah, not even, I-"

"I'm playing with you Kei'. I understand what you saying. We would be all angry putting books away in Mrs. Turner's, giving each other the silent treatment." We both laugh again. "Um, I know what I just said about being your girl and all, but..." She glances out the window and then back at me.

"But what?" I ask as I lean forward.

"This is going to sound weird, but maybe we can be 'unofficially official.'"

"It don't sound weird at all. 'Unofficially official,' I like that."

ABOUT THE AUTHOR

R. A. Ingram is an educator from San Jose, CA. He lives with his wife and Chihuahua and has a passion for social justice and the arts. He works in an economically and socially underserved community. His passion for writing stems from the fact that people of color are misrepresented or left out of young adult fiction. His ultimate goal is to motivate and mentor young people to write their own stories and share them with the world.

Made in the USA
Monee, IL
18 June 2020